Mrs Pepperpot at the Bazaar

A Red Fox Book

Published by Random House Children's Books
20 Vauxhall Bridge Road, London SW1V 2SA

A division of The Random House Group Ltd
London Melbourne Sydney Auckland Johannesburg
and agencies throughout the world

1 3 5 7 9 10 8 6 4 2

First published in Great Britain by
Hutchinson Children's Books 1987
Red Fox edition 1989
This Red Fox edition 2000

Printed in Singapore by Tien Wah Press (PTE) Ltd

The Random House Group Limited Reg. No. 954009

www.randomhouse.co.uk

ISBN 0 09 959760 8

Mrs Pepperpot at the Bazaar

Alf Prøysen

Illustrated by David Arthur

One day Mrs Pepperpot was alone in her kitchen. At least, she was not *quite* alone, because Hannah was there as well. She was busy scraping out a bowl and licking the spoon, for the old woman had been making gingerbread shapes.

There was a knock at the door. Mrs Pepperpot said, 'Come in.' And in walked three very smart ladies.

'Good afternoon,' said the smart ladies. 'We are collecting prizes for the lottery at the school bazaar this evening. Do you think you have some little thing we could have? The money from the bazaar is for the boys' brass band – they need new instruments.'

'Oh, I'd like to help with that,' said Mrs Pepperpot, for she dearly loved brass bands.

'Would a plate of gingerbread be any use?'

'Of course,' said the smart ladies, but they laughed behind her back. 'We could take it with us now if you have it ready,' they said. But Mrs Pepperpot wanted to go to the bazaar herself, so she said she would bring the gingerbread.

So the three smart ladies went away and Mrs Pepperpot was very proud and pleased that she was going to a bazaar.

Hannah was still scraping away at the bowl and licking the sweet mixture from the spoon.

'May I come with you?' she asked.

'Certainly, if your father and mother will let you.'

'I'm sure they will,' said the child, 'because Father has to work at the factory and Mother is at her sewing all day.'

'Be here at six o'clock then,' said Mrs Pepperpot, and started making another batch of gingerbread shapes.

But when Hannah came back at six the old woman was not there. All the doors were open, so she went from room to room, calling her. When she got back to the kitchen she heard an odd noise coming from the table. The mixing bowl was upside down, so she lifted it carefully. And there underneath sat her friend who was now as small as a pepperpot.

'Isn't this a nuisance?' said Mrs Pepperpot. 'I was just cleaning out the bowl after putting the gingerbread in the oven when I suddenly started shrinking. Then the bowl turned over on me.

Quick! Get the cakes out of the oven before they burn!'

But it was too late; the gingerbread was burnt to a cinder.

Mrs Pepperpot sat down and cried, she was so disappointed. But she soon gave that up and started thinking instead. Suddenly she laughed out loud and said:

'Hannah! Put me under the tap and give me a good wash. We're going to the bazaar, you and I!'

'But you can't go to the bazaar like that!' said Hannah.

'Oh yes, I can,' said Mrs Pepperpot, 'as long as you do what I say.'

Hannah promised, but Mrs Pepperpot gave her some very strange orders.

First she was to fetch a silk ribbon and tie it round the old woman so that it looked like a skirt. Then she was to fetch some tinsel from the Christmas decorations. This she had to wind round and round to make a silver bodice. And lastly she had to make a bonnet of gold foil.

'Now you must wrap me carefully in paper and put me in a cardboard box,' said Mrs Pepperpot.

'Why?' asked Hannah.

'When I've promised them a prize for the bazaar they must have it,' said Mrs Pepperpot, 'so I'm giving them myself. Just put me down on one of the tables and say you've brought a mechanical doll. Tell them you keep the key in your pocket and then pretend to wind me up so that people can see how clever I am.'

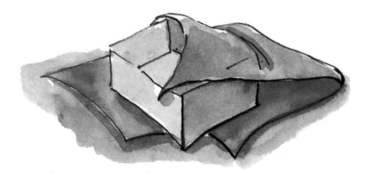

Hannah did as she was told, and when she got to the bazaar and put the wonderful doll on the table, many people clapped their hands and crowded round to see.

'What a pretty doll!' they said. 'And what a lovely dress!'

'Look at her gold bonnet!'

Mrs Pepperpot lay absolutely still in her cardboard box, but when she heard how everybody praised her, she winked at Hannah with one eye, and Hannah knew what she wanted. She lifted Mrs Pepperpot very carefully out of the box and pretended to wind her up at the back with a key.

Everyone was watching her. But when Mrs Pepperpot began walking across the table, picking her way through the prizes, there was great excitement.

'Look, the doll can walk!'

And when Mrs Pepperpot began to dance they started shouting and yelling with delight, 'The doll is dancing!'

The three smart ladies who had been to see Mrs Pepperpot earlier in the day sat in special seats and looked very grand. One of them had given six expensive coffee cups, the second an elegant table mat and the third a beautiful iced layer cake.

Mrs Pepperpot decided to go over and speak to them, for she was afraid they had recognized her and thought it odd that she hadn't brought the gingerbread.

The three smart ladies were very pleased when the doll came walking across the table to them.

'Come to me!' said the one who had given the coffee cups, and stretched her hand out towards Mrs Pepperpot, who walked on to it obediently.

'Let me hold her a little,' said the lady with the elegant table mat, and Mrs Pepperpot went over to her hand.

'Now it's my turn,' said the lady with the iced cake.

I'm sure they know it's me, thought Mrs Pepperpot, that's why they stare at me so hard and hold me on their hands.

But then the lady with the cake said, 'Well, I must say, this is a much better prize than the gingerbread that the odd old woman offered us today.'

Now she should never have said that; Mrs Pepperpot leaped straight out of her hand and landed PLOP right in the middle of the beautiful iced layer cake.

Then she got up and waded right through it.
The cake lady screamed, but people were shouting
with laughter by now.

'Take that doll away!' shrieked the second lady,
but *squish*, *squash* went Mrs Pepperpot's sticky
feet, right across her lovely table mat.

'Get that dreadful doll away!' cried the third lady.

But it was too late; Mrs Pepperpot was on the tray with the expensive coffee cups, and began to dance a jig. Cups and saucers flew about and broke in little pieces.

What a to-do! The conductor of the brass band had quite a job to quieten them all down. He announced that the winning numbers of the lottery would be given out.

'First prize will be the wonderful mechanical doll,' he said.

When Hannah heard that, she was very frightened. What would happen if somebody won Mrs Pepperpot, so that she couldn't go home to her husband? She tugged at Mrs Pepperpot's skirt and whispered, 'Shall I put you in my pocket and creep away?'

'No,' said Mrs Pepperpot.

'But think how awful it would be if someone won you and took you home.'

'What must be must be!' said Mrs Pepperpot.

The conductor called out the winning number, 'Three hundred and eleven!' Everyone looked at their tickets, but no one had number three hundred and eleven.

'That's a good thing!' sighed Hannah with relief.
There would have to be another draw. But just then
she remembered she had a ticket in her hand; it
was number three hundred and eleven!

'Wait!' she cried, and showed her ticket. The
conductor looked at it and saw it was the right one.

So Hannah was allowed to take Mrs Pepperpot
home.

Next day the old woman was her proper size again and Hannah only a little girl, and Mrs Pepperpot said, 'You're my little girl, aren't you?'

'Yes,' said Hannah, 'and you're my very own Mrs Pepperpot, because I won you at the bazaar yesterday.'

And that was the end of Mrs Pepperpot's adventures for a very long time.